First edition
2 4 6 8 10 9 7 5 3 1

Library of Congress Cataloging-in-Publication Data

The gingerbread man : a classic fairy tale / illustrated by Dominique Thibault ;
[translated by Molly Stevens]. — 1st ed.
p. cm. — (Little pebbles)
Summary: A freshly baked gingerbread man escapes when he is taken out of the oven and
eludes a number of hungry animals until he meets a clever fox.
ISBN 0-7892-0733-8 (alk. paper)
[1. Fairy Tales. 2. Folklore.] I. Thibault, Dominique, ill.
II. Stevens, Molly. III. Gingerbread boy. English. IV. Series
PZ8.G3977 2001
398.21—dc21
[E]   2001022485

The Gingerbread Man

A Classic Fairy Tale
Illustrated by Dominique Thibault

· Abbeville Kids ·
A Division of Abbeville Publishing Group
New York · London

There was once an old woman who was making gingerbread. She had some dough left over, so she shaped it into a gingerbread man that she could eat later as her afternoon snack.

With raisins she made two little eyes, a smiling mouth, and three buttons for his jacket. Then she put him into the oven to bake.

Soon the smell of baking gingerbread filled the house, and the old woman heard knocking from inside the oven. When she opened the oven door, the Gingerbread Man hopped out and ran out of the house.

"Come back here!" cried the old woman. "I made you for my afternoon snack!"

But the Gingerbread Man yelled back,

"Run, run, as fast as you can!

You can't catch me,

I'm the Gingerbread Man!"

The old woman chased him into the garden, where her husband was working. His eyes widened in surprise as he saw the Gingerbread Man run by and then his wife chasing after him.

"Stop him!" she shouted. "I made him for my snack!"

The old man tried to catch him, but the Gingerbread Man ran past him shouting,

"Run, run, as fast as you can!

You can't catch me,

I'm the Gingerbread Man!"

When he got to the road, the Gingerbread Man met a cow.

"Stop!" she called out. "You look delicious!"

But the Gingerbread Man just kept on running. He yelled over his shoulder,

"I've run from an old woman,

I've run from an old man.

Run, run, as fast as you can!

You can't catch me,

I'm the Gingerbread Man!"

The cow started to chase him. Just behind her were the old man and the old woman.

Next the Gingerbread Man met a horse.
"Stop!" cried the horse. "I want to eat you!"
But the Gingerbread Man answered,
"I've run from an old woman,
I've run from an old man,
I've run from a cow.
Run, run, as fast as you can!
You can't catch me,
I'm the Gingerbread Man!"
So the horse started chasing the Gingerbread Man,
along with the cow, the old man, and the old woman.

Down the road the Gingerbread Man came to some peasants who were gathering up the hay. When they smelled the warm gingerbread, they cried, "Stop! We want to eat you!"

But the Gingerbread Man called back,

"I've run from an old woman,
I've run from an old man,
I've run from a cow,
I've run from a horse.
Run, run, as fast as you can!
You can't catch me,
I'm the Gingerbread Man!"

At that the peasants joined all the others who were chasing the Gingerbread Man: the horse, the cow, the old man, and the old woman.

The Gingerbread Man ran past a fox in a field, and called out to him,

"Run, run, as fast as you can!

You can't catch me,

I'm the Gingerbread Man!"

The fox thought the Gingerbread Man smelled delicious, but he sighed, "I don't feel like running. Besides, I never eat gingerbread. It's bad for my teeth."

The Gingerbread Man had only gone a few more steps when he came to a river. The fox saw the peasants, the horse, the cow, the old man, and the old woman running toward them. So he said to the Gingerbread Man, "Hop on and I'll take you across the river."

"How do I know you won't eat me?" asked the Gingerbread Man.

"If you get on my tail, I won't be able to eat you," the sly fox answered.

So the Gingerbread Man got on the fox's tail and the fox began swimming across the river. Soon the fox's tail was dragging in the water, so the Gingerbread Man climbed onto the fox's back. When they got to the middle of the river, the fox said, "You'd better get on my head, if you want to stay dry."

The Gingerbread Man stood on top of the fox's head, but the current was very strong and the fox's head was bobbing up and down in the water.

"Climb onto my nose, if you don't want to fall off and drown," said the fox. So the Gingerbread Man slid down onto the fox's nose.

But as soon as he did, the fox opened his mouth and gobbled up the Gingerbread Man.

The fox sat down on the riverbank and smugly looked at the peasants, the horse, the cow, the old man, and the old woman on the other side of the river.

He licked his chops and said,

"Run, run, as fast as you can!

If you can catch me,

You'll have the Gingerbread Man!"

Look carefully at these pictures from the story.
They're all mixed up. Can you put them back in the
right order?

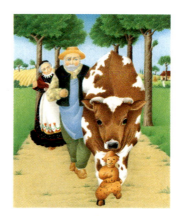

What does the Gingerbread Man say to everyone he meets?

Run, run, as fast as you can!
You can't catch me,
I'm the Gingerbread Man!